On the
TRAPPING TRAIL

Written by Neil and Ting Morris
Illustrated by Anna Clarke
Historical advisor: Marion Wood

Evans Brothers Limited

Published by Evans Brothers Limited
2A Portman Mansions, Chiltern Street
London W1M 1LE

First published 1988

Printed in Hong Kong by Wing King Tong Co. Ltd.

ISBN 0 237 50970 9

INTRODUCTION

A new nation was born in 1783 when the Revolutionary War ended and the United States gained independence. At that time the western boundary was formed by the Mississippi River. Beyond that was a vast wilderness, the home of wild animals and nomadic tribes of Plains Indians.

In 1803 the United States made the Louisiana Purchase, buying over 2 million square kilometres of land from the French. For an agreed sum of 15 million dollars, this deal more than doubled the territory of the previous 17 states of the young republic. The new land stretched westwards from the Mississippi to the Rocky Mountains. Soon daring pioneers and fur trappers started forging trails into the forests, mountains and deserts of this unmapped new territory.

When Texas joined the United States, cowboys began driving huge herds of longhorn cattle northwards. The age of Wild West towns had arrived, and with it the rush for gold in California. This is the image of the American West that has lived on for over a hundred years, kept alive by legends and Hollywood westerns. Between 1810 and 1840 the great fur trade boom attracted many to become trappers. In their search for beaver streams they became the courageous explorers who opened the land to the pioneers and settlers. Their enemies were wild animals, hostile Indians and ruthless rivals. Each year in early summer the trappers met together to sell their furs and stock up with fresh supplies.

This story is about one trapper and his son, and their adventures in the wild. The information pages with the rifle border will tell you more about the life and work of the trappers of the American West.

As the boat went up river, Jake watched his home town
slowly disappear. He was the only youngster among the
fur trappers, but he had learned a lot from his father's
hunting stories. Jake had always known that one day he
would go with him on the trapping trail.

When his mother died, Jake had told his father that he was old enough to go with him. 'It's hard and dangerous,' Joe warned his son. Joe was one of the best beaver trappers in the West, and he usually worked on his own. But he knew Jake would be a companion he could trust.

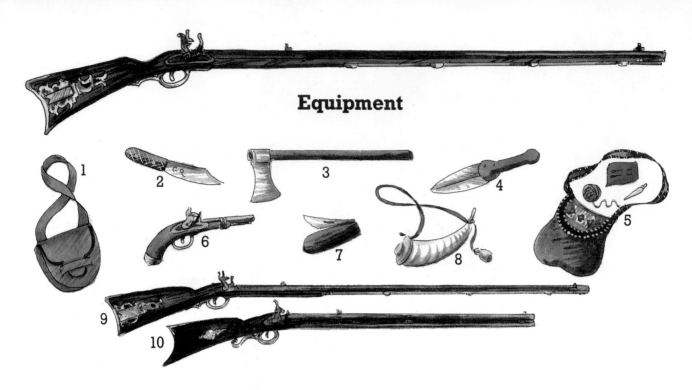

Equipment

Trappers were also called mountain men, because they set their traps in the rivers and streams of the Rocky Mountains. Theirs was a lonely, dangerous life. They admired Indian skills and copied many of their ways.

Equipment: 1 bullet pouch; 2 Green River knife; 3 axe; 4 dagger; 5 possibles bag containing needles, awl and twine; 6 percussion cap pistol; 7 folding knife; 8 powder horn; 9 Kentucky rifle; 10 double-barrelled Plains rifle.

A) Trappers lit fires by hitting flint with a striker; the sparks caught the punk – rotten wood which trappers used as tinder.

B) Bullets were made of lead. Molten lead was poured into a metal mould which opened to give round bullets. These were carried in the trappers' bullet pouch.

As they moved upstream, the land grew more wild.
Suddenly they saw smoke signals. 'We are in Crow
country,' Joe told his son. 'But we needn't fear the Indians,
the Crow chief is my friend.' They moved on into the hills.

At the Crow camp Chief Hawkface made the travellers welcome. He was happy to trade two of his horses for knives and mirrors.

Little Wolf, the chief's son, showed Jake the Indian way of hunting. Before leaving, Jake gave him one of his best knives, and Little Wolf made a gift of his bow and arrow. Now they were brothers.

Joe led them over mountains that no man had ever travelled. One evening as they were looking for a good place to camp, a cub joined them. Jake wanted to pick it up, but he felt his father's hand stopping him.

Seconds later a puma sprang from nowhere, picked up her cub and was gone. When Jake looked at his father, his finger was still on the trigger.

Their journey took them many weeks. Following the creeks and streams, they at last found beaver dams and lodges. They set their traps and waited. Joe knew from experience that this would be a good place to trap.

Beaver trapping

Beavers live on land and in water. Using their chisel-like teeth, they cut down trees both for food and to build dams and lodges. They live in the lodge, which they make out of branches and stones pasted together with mud. The entrance is below water so that other animals cannot get inside, but the lodge itself is quite dry.

Trappers caught beavers in steel traps chained to stakes under water. When the beaver was caught in the trap, it drowned. The beaver skins were stretched on willow frame hoops, pressed and sold in packs to fur traders. In the 19th century beaver fur was very fashionable for hats and trimmings.

Every day they made an excellent catch. There were so
many good trapping streams that they decided to build
their winter cabin here. Jake soon became an expert
bowman.

They took turns hunting for food. One day Joe said, 'I've
seen moose tracks in the forest. Tonight we'll have a feast!'

Housing and hunting

Trappers often made winter camp in a log hut or cabin. Or they would live in a tent made of skins on a frame of wooden poles, with a smoke hole at the top. They carried as little as possible apart from their blankets, but usually took salt and flour with them.

bobcat
beaver
buffalo
mink
hawk
rabbit
moose
fox
caribou
wolf

Trappers hunted many animals for meat. Beaver, mink and fox were very popular for their fur.

Joe tracked the moose through the forest. Suddenly he came face to face with a great grizzly bear. He had no time to use his rifle, but suddenly there was a noise in the trees. Was it the moose? The grizzly raised itself to its full height and turned. Joe pushed past and ran.

Joe was a good runner, but he had never run as fast before.
When he knew he was safe, he turned to look for the
grizzly. But it had gone.

It was only then that he saw the blood. Hours later Jake
went in search of his father. He found him exhausted and in
pain. It was turning colder and starting to snow.

It took them a long time to make their way back. As they neared home, Joe sensed danger. 'Don't move!' he whispered. Hostile Blackfoot surrounded their cabin. They could only watch as the Indians robbed them of their

horses and pelts.

Sign language

hello

trade

friend

me

summer

winter

horserider

kill

white man

Crow

Apache

Blackfoot

Indian tribes spoke different languages. So they used sign language to communicate with each other. These hand signals were learned by the trappers and explorers who first met and traded with the Indians. Between each sign the speaker returns his hands to his side to show it is finished.

Joe's wounds healed quickly, and they were soon trapping again. Before long they had made up for all the stolen pelts.

When the spring thaw came, they made a canoe to carry their pelts. They would soon be off to sell them at the great meeting.

It was hard going. Each time they came to strong rapids or a waterfall, they unloaded the canoe and carried it. It took weeks to reach the great meeting place.

Trading posts

Trappers often used a fort as their base. Here they sold their furs and stocked up with fresh supplies. Indians who traded their furs camped outside the fort. Fort Laramie was one of the most important trading posts in the Rocky Mountains, and it was later taken over by the American Fur Company.

A great meeting – or 'rendezvous' – was held every year in late spring at an agreed place. As well as being an opportunity for trading, this was a very festive occasion. There was bartering, wrestling and shooting matches, singing and dancing. The trappers spent most of the money they got for their furs on drink and gambling.

Jake and his father had been on their own for almost a year. After all this time it would be good to meet friends again.

Jake spent some time with Little Wolf while his father sold their furs. 'When we've sold everything,' Joe said to his son, 'you must make your decision.'

Jake had decided about his future long before this. They got a good price for their furs and bought new traps and equipment. And as the days passed, Jake longed to return to the great mountains to find new trapping trails.

This map of the American West shows the rivers and streams where the mountain men hunted and trapped.

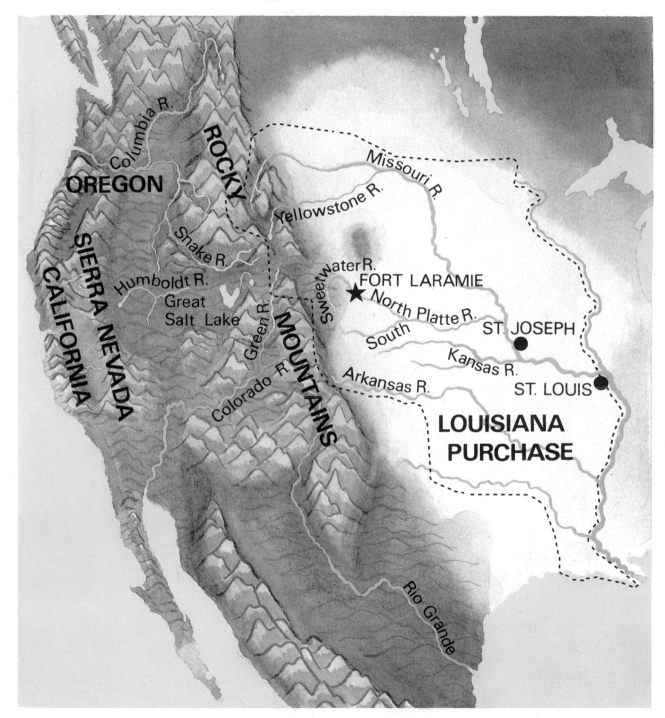